Captain James Cook

Betty Lou Kratoville

High Noon Books
Novato, California

Cover Photo: North Wind Picture Archives
Interior Illustrations: North Wind Picture Archives
Pictorial History Research

International Standard Book Number: 1-57128-170-3

9 8 7 6 5 4 3 2
0 9 8 7 6 5 4 3 2

Contents

CHAPTER 1

The Right Man

In the 1700s England badly needed new colonies. There were many reasons for this. The settlers in America were about to revolt. French and Spanish explorers were on the move. Their ships sailed all over the world. They wanted to find new lands before England could get there first. Then they could claim these new lands for *their* countries. In a way, it was a race.

King George III of England had a group of men who gave him advice. They all said he should send out an expedition to seek new lands. They did not want England to fall behind France and Spain.

They also had another reason. They knew that the Planet Venus would pass between the earth and the sun in June of 1769. Men of science were eager to watch this rare event. A good place to see it was the South Pacific. King George agreed with them. He also hoped that new lands would be found on such a voyage – new lands that could be claimed for England.

Who would lead this voyage? Naval officers of high rank looked long and hard. At last they found just the right man for the job. His name was James Cook. At that time he was a lieutenant in the navy. It would be years before he would be made a captain. But now he was in command of an important voyage. So he was referred to as *Captain* Cook.

Who was this man? His family had always been poor. His father worked on a farm. There was never any extra money. James went to school for only a few years. Then he had to get a job to help his family. He first worked for a grocer, then for the owner of a general store. For a while he had a job on a ship that carried coal from one port to another. He liked life aboard ship, so he decided to join the navy. His family could not understand it. In those days the life of a seaman was hard. Food was bad and there was not much of it. Living and sleeping space was cramped. Rules were strict. Punishment was harsh. But James had made up his mind. He joined the English navy. In two years he had become a master. That meant he was in full charge of running a ship.

He took part in the French and Indian wars. He became expert at drawing maps of lands that at that time had no maps. He was also good at math and astronomy. He seemed to have a sharp mind for business. All together these strong points brought him command of the ship *Endeavor*. The *Endeavor* was not a beautiful ship but it was a sturdy one. Even so, certain changes had to be made for such a long journey. Cabins were built for Cook and his officers. Three small boats to get them from the ship to shore were needed. Eight tons of iron for ballast were brought on board to steady the ship in rough seas.

At first the *Endeavor* seemed to have enough space. That was important for the trip was expected to last two years. Much had to be loaded on board. Food, tools, arms, gifts for friendly or unfriendly natives, lots of equipment for scientists.

Cook knew how to plan well. But now and then there was a snag. He was told he had to make room for the scientist Joseph Banks and his four servants. Then two more scientists and two artists came on board. They all seemed to have tons of baggage, instruments, books, and two dogs! What to do? Cook and his officers gave up their cabins and moved their bunks below deck. Somehow space was made for everyone and everything.

Cook had orders to sail southward. Surely there was land never before seen that could be claimed for King George. To claim a new land, one needed only to plant his country's flag. Or one could firmly attach a note with date and explorer's name to a tree or stone.

At last all was ready. The *Endeavor* set sail from Plymouth, England, on August 26, 1768.

CHAPTER 2

The First Voyage (1768-1771) – Part I

The *Endeavor's* first stop was the island of
Madeira. This island lay off the north coast of
Africa. The stop had been planned. Cook needed
to take on fresh fruit, vegetables, and beef for his
crew. Fresh water was vital. And so was wine
because stored water tended to get stale. Then it
had a bad taste.

The next stop at Rio de Janeiro in South
America in November was not a success. A
viceroy ruled the city. He was sure that the

Endeavor's men were all spies. No one could change his mind. He would not let Joseph Banks collect plants. But Banks did not give up. He bribed the soldiers sent to guard the ship. In this way he was able to sneak onto the shore at night. Once there he quickly gathered plants and shrubs. Cook badly wanted to leave this unfriendly place but storms kept him there for 26 days.

They reached the southern tip of South America in January. The crew had been told they would find giants there. Not a single giant was to be found. Just plain men and women living in tumble-down shacks.

Banks took a group on shore to look for plant life. They were caught in a sudden snowstorm. By morning two of Banks's servants had died from the bitter cold. The rest barely made it back to the ship.

It was time to move on. Great danger lay ahead. Many ships had been wrecked as they tried to sail around Cape Horn. The waves were huge. Violent storms raged one after another.

Captain Cook was lucky, and he was skilled. He made the trip around the Horn in only 33 days. It was during this stage of the trip that the crew had its first taste of albatross, the huge bird with a 10-15 foot wing span. Mr. Banks said the bird had a good flavor as long as it was cooked with a tasty sauce.

After Cape Horn, Cook spent weeks

searching for new land in the most remote stretch of the South Pacific. Nothing! So he turned his ship northwest. In April the *Endeavor* reached Tahiti. It was a paradise! A bright, fair climate. Plentiful fruit and fish. Natives who made them welcome.

The Tahitians had one bad habit. If they saw something they liked, they took it. This did not seem like stealing to them. But that is what it seemed like to Captain Cook and his crew.

At times there was anger on both sides. The Tahitians had temples. They called them *maraes*. One day some men from the *Endeavor* took some stones from a marae to use for ballast. The islanders were upset. Captain Cook made his men

Captain Cook trades with natives.

put the stones back. Most of the time it was just a case of one culture not able to understand another culture.

Some of the native customs did seem very odd to the Englishmen. For example, a chief had to be carried at all times. His feet could never touch the ground. He had to be fed by hand by servants. Roasted dog was a favorite food. Women were not allowed to eat with men. Sometimes native priests smothered their own children. It was all very strange.

A camp was set up on the beach. Here the scientists waited for the day when Venus would move between the earth and the sun. Alas! There was a haze around the planet on that day. Nothing could be seen.

Before leaving Tahiti, Captain Cook mapped its coast. He planted the English flag on some nearby islands and named them the Society Islands. Then he turned the *Endeavor* south. New lands were waiting to be discovered. He would try again. This time surely he would succeed!

CHAPTER 3

The First Voyage (1768-1771) – Part II

Two months later the *Endeavor* reached New Zealand. This wild country had been found by a Dutchman in 1642 but he had not gone ashore. Cook and his men were the first people from Europe to set foot on New Zealand.

The first meeting with the New Zealanders did not go well. The natives were terrified of these strange white men. Their "thunder sticks" flashed lightning that could kill. Cook tried to make friends with the frightened tribes. After a while he gave up. Before he left, he raised an English flag and claimed the land for King George III.

The next step was to circle New Zealand. From time to time the crew went ashore. Joseph Banks was thrilled. There were so many growing things he had never seen. Cook was surprised by the language of the natives, who were called Maoris. They spoke much like the people of Tahiti. How could this be? Tahiti was 2,000 miles away.

The biggest shock came when the Englishmen learned the Maoris were cannibals. They did not eat their enemies because of hate or hunger. They ate them to soak up their strength and courage!

After six months Cook knew that New Zealand was not the new land he sought. He headed west to Australia. Other men had spotted Australia but felt it was worthless. No colonists would want to settle in this strange, ugly place.

The *Endeavor* dropped its anchor on the east coast of Australia. The people were not friendly. Yet they were not unfriendly. They did not want the white men's beads, nails, mirrors, and other gifts. It seemed as if they simply wanted the strangers to go away.

Once again Banks found dozens of new plants. The land was so rich and fertile, Cook named the harbor Botany Bay.

One day while sailing on the coast, the

Endeavor got stuck on a reef. (That reef is now known as the Great Barrier Reef all over the world.) Water gushed into the ship. The men worked the pumps for 36 straight hours. Ballast was heaved overboard. At last a high tide lifted the *Endeavor* off the reef. A sail was used to plug the hole in the bottom of the ship until it could be fixed.

Cook docked the ship as quickly as he could. The crew set to work. It took six weeks to make the *Endeavor* safe to sail in again. During these busy days the Englishmen were amazed by some strange animals. One had a long tail, made gigantic leaps, and carried its young in a pocket!

Captain Cook vowed that his crew would stay

17

healthy. He made them eat beef every day as well as orange and lemon syrup. He even forced them to eat sauerkraut! At first they hated it. But these foods were all rich in vitamin C. They kept the sailors from getting scurvy.

All this changed when the ship reached Batavia on the way home. It was a filthy city. Sewers were open. Canals were choked with garbage. Disease was everywhere. In less than two weeks Cook and Banks were very ill. Crew members were either sick or too weak to work. Cook left Batavia as soon as repairs to the ship had been made. Not a moment too soon! So many seamen had died that Cook had to stop in Cape Town, South Africa, to hire more men.

Two years and eleven months after leaving home, the *Endeavor* returned to England. Cook had not yet found a new continent in the South Pacific. But his maps and charts won high praise. The English people listened wide-eyed when he told his tales of Pacific natives and their strange ways.

CHAPTER 4

The Second Voyage (1772-1775) – Part I

The voyage of the *Endeavor* brought great fame to Joseph Banks. People waited in line to see the 1,000 rare plants he had collected. And the dried human head! And the strange insects. And other odd things never before seen in England – native weapons, clothing, and food. He brought a crown of gold and bright feathers for King George. The king loved it.

What about Captain Cook? After a few weeks, interest dropped off. People no longer sought him out. The worst news was that two of his children had died while he was at sea. It was a sad time for Cook and his wife.

After a short leave he was ordered to report to the naval chiefs in London. These men had poured over his new maps and journals. They knew good work when they saw it. They were even more impressed by the fact that Cook's ship had been free of scurvy. Until this time, scurvy had simply been a fact of life on board all ships.

It was clear to all that Cook was the man to command a second voyage. Of course, Cook thought so, too. This time he was to have two ships. One was called the *Resolution*. The other was called the *Adventure*. Good names for ships that were setting out to explore the unknown world!

Joseph Banks badly wanted to join this expedition. Every effort was made to find space for him. But his staff was large. His equipment was bulky. There simply was not room on either ship. Banks was disappointed but he and Cook stayed friends. Cook found other scientists to go with him. They would study the heavens and the seas. He invited artists to join him to make drawings of people, places, animals, and plants.

The two ships left Plymouth, England, on July 13, 1772. It was just a year and a day since the *Endeavor's* return from the first voyage. Cook was captain of the *Resolution*. A man named

Tobias Furneaux commanded the *Adventure*.
Twenty sailors from the *Endeavor's* first trip asked
to sign up for another voyage. Cook was glad to
have them.

Once again Cook was ordered to look for a
continent at the "bottom of the world." The two
ships sailed straight into strange frozen waters.
They saw icebergs and whales and penguins. But,
as far as Cook could tell, no continent. Just great
walls of solid ice.

Drinking water ran low. Cook sent seamen
out in boats to hack off chunks of ice to melt in
huge copper pots. Why, they all wondered, was
the melted water not salty? They did not know
that the ice was not frozen sea water. It was

pressed snow from slowly-moving glaciers.

It was a hard life. Sails froze. Ropes turned hard and brittle. Hands were frostbitten. Seamen grew numb with cold. Cook decided it was time to move on. He headed back to New Zealand. The ships needed repairs. The crews needed rest, fresh food, and water.

When they reached New Zealand, Cook grew angry. He learned that many of Captain Furneaux's men had scurvy. It was clear that Furneaux had not watched his men's diet. Cook sent a group of men to search for plants he knew were rich in vitamin C. He ordered that these be eaten every day along with grains. The scurvy soon vanished.

Three months later the ships tried again to find a new continent. Once again they failed. Cook turned his ships to Tahiti. There had been two wars since the *Endeavor's* visit. Cook found that a lot of his native friends had been killed. Somehow the island paradise was not the same. The ships moved onto other islands. Then back to New Zealand and yet another try at finding a new continent.

Furneaux sent ten men ashore to gather greens. He waited and waited. They did not come back. Then he found out that all of them had been killed and *eaten*. He was so horrified that he turned the *Resolution* around and went home to England just as fast as he could get there!

CHAPTER 5

The Second Voyage (1772-1775) – Part II

Now Cook was alone. He crossed the Antarctic Circle twice. Twice he had to turn back. He could not get his ship through the ice. Some of the seamen grew ill. Cook himself had not felt well for a few weeks. In his journals he wrote that he gained back his strength by eating his own pet dog!

Cook was sure he had sailed farther south than any man before him. He planned to try again the following year. Meanwhile he headed for a place on an old map called Easter Island. Here he and his crew were amazed by the gigantic stone heads 15 to 35 feet high! Some weighed as much as 50 tons. How these heads had been built and moved around the island hundreds of years ago without modern tools is still a mystery today.

The next stop was the Marquesas Islands. The land there was lush and rich. The people were handsome and friendly. They loved red parrot feathers. Luckily, Cook had a large supply of these on the *Resolution*. He traded them for fish, fruit, and pigs.

On to Tahiti. No longer a good place to be! The Tahitians were getting ready to go to war with neighbors on a nearly island. Thousands of natives carried clubs and stones. Dozens and dozens of war canoes were lined up on the shore. They wanted Cook to join them. He said no.

It was time to head south. On the way they explored many islands. The natives in some of them were so friendly that Cook hated to leave. But he had to think about the weather. He must make his final try to find a southern continent during the warm months.

He made a quick stop in New Zealand. Then Cook made up his mind to explore the South Atlantic once more. Alas! No sign of a new continent there. Now and then the ship passed an island. Cook could not land his small boats on any of them because of ice.

Was there a southern continent? Maybe. Maybe not. At last Cook decided that even if he found land, no one could settle there. Too much snow and ice. Too short a season for growing things. In fact, could anything at all ever grow there? He stopped the search and set sail for England.

Cook may not have found a southern continent. But he made huge gains in the knowledge of world geography. The Pacific Ocean had never been fully explored. Cook explored vast areas of it. Until then, no one knew how huge this ocean was. No one knew that it covered one third of the world. Or that it was twice as large as the Atlantic Ocean. Or that it was bigger than all the land surfaces put together.

He found new lands. He brought news of people never heard of before. And he convinced everyone that there was no rich southern continent that kept the earth from flying off into space!

He also proved that on a journey of more than 70,000 miles, not one man needed to die of scurvy.

CHAPTER 6

The Third Voyage (1776-1789) – Part I

The second voyage ended but no one seemed to care. King George had his mind on other things. The colonies in America had started to revolt. The king had to send his troops to try and stop it.

Perhaps Captain Cook did not get a lot of praise from the English people. But men of high rank in the navy thought well of him. They gave him a medal for his fight against scurvy. At long last they raised his rank to captain. They also found him an easy job as head of a hospital for old seamen. Now he could live at home with his wife and sons. He would have time to write a book about life on the high seas. It sounded good. But, to tell the truth, the job bored him.

One day Cook heard that the navy had plans for a third trip to the Pacific. He quickly let them know that he would like to lead it. They agreed just as quickly. But, they said, no more searches for a new continent. This time he was to find the Northwest Passage. They wanted a waterway north of Canada that would connect the Atlantic and Pacific oceans. Men had searched for such a passage for years.

Why? Because England needed a fast trade route to China's tea and silk trade. Also, a

Northwest Passage might make up for lost trade with the American colonies. It was so important, the king had offered a large reward to the man who found it. Many men had tried. None had met success.

The Americans declared their independence on July 4, 1776. Eight days later two ships left England. Cook was again in command of the *Resolution* with a crew of 112 men. By now it was a leaky old tub. Still it stayed afloat and seemed to get the job done.

Charles Clerke commanded the *Discovery* with 70 men. The *Discovery* was a sound, strong ship. Clerke was a sound, strong commander.

First stop: Cape Town, South Africa. Next

stop: Kerguelen's Island about 2,000 miles southeast. Third stop: Tasmania, a bleak and friendless island. Then a detour to the Friendly Islands after a short stay in New Zealand.

The Friendly Islands deserved their name. Captain Cook and his crew were given a warm welcome. Pasture for their livestock was plentiful. The English settled down for a long stay.

One of the island chiefs boarded the *Resolution*. At first he would not walk downstairs into Cook's cabin. He did not want people to "walk on my head."

The islanders brought gifts of food and animals. They danced and sang while drums beat.

Captain Cook lands on the Friendly Islands.

35

It was a holiday for the hard-working seamen.

Only one thing worried the men. Captain Cook had changed. He punished the islanders for innocent mischief. His harsh punishment did not seem to match their light-hearted fun. He never laughed and seldom smiled. Was he unwell? Tired? No one seemed to know.

Now it was time to look for the Northwest Passage. On the way to the American coast, Cook sighted the Hawaiian Islands. The natives there were stunned by the huge sailing ships. And the men with light skins. And their strange "sticks of wood" (guns). Cook found their language much like that of the Tahitians. How strange! Tahiti was 3,000 miles away.

The ships reached the American coast in rough weather. Sleet, snow, and wind kept them from landing. They did make an important stop farther north at Vancouver Island. The people there were dressed in furs. Cook was headed for frigid weather. His men had to have warm clothes. Trading was brisk. The natives wanted anything made of metal. The seamen wanted furs. A good exchange!

The ships sailed on through winter storms. Cook's old maps were often wrong. Now the land veered west instead of north. Sometimes a hopeful inlet proved to be a dead end. Where in the world was the Northwest Passage?

CHAPTER 7

The Third Voyage (1776-1780) – Part II

The ships reached the Aleutian Islands. Cook spent little time there. He wasn't eager to meet nearby Russian traders. Instead he headed for the Bering Sea. From there the ships sailed into the Arctic Ocean.

It was a dark, gloomy voyage. The fog was thick and blinding. Tons of ice drifting toward the ships were a constant danger. One day the final blow fell! A thick wall of ice blocked their way. They could do nothing but turn back.

Captain Cook was careful to draw new maps of these regions. He kept daily journals that told of the land, its climate, people, and animals.

Since they could go no farther, they headed for Hawaii's warm sun. It took seven weeks to find a harbor off the large island of Hawaii.

Captain Cook was amazed. Thousands of people lived on this island — more than he had ever seen on any other island. A high priest came aboard ship. He called Cook "Lono." Lono was a Hawaiian god who, it was thought, brought peace and good times. Lono came during a sacred season from October to January.

Cook had sailed in during these sacred months, so he must be Lono. He was worshiped as a god. The natives held ceremonies in his honor. Some were a bit hard to take such as eating the minced pig that a chief had already chewed!

To the natives the *Resolution* was a sacred floating island. Kings and priests came aboard bringing gifts. They made sure their people helped the seamen haul heavy loads. Even with all this good feeling, the chiefs were glad when the ships left. Feeding the Englishmen had put a great strain on their own food supply.

Their relief did not last long. The two ships were badly damaged in a sudden storm and had to return to Hawaii. This time the Hawaiians seemed to resent their return. The sacred season was over. Why had Lono come back? Perhaps he was not a

Death of Captain Cook

god after all.

Now the natives were downright rude. They made threats when seamen tried to get fresh water. In turn, Cook grew angry. He ordered his men to load their guns. One day fighting broke out. The natives attacked with clubs and spears and knives. The seamen grabbed their guns.

And then disaster! Cook was hit from behind with a club. Then he was stabbed in the back. He fell into the water. He was stabbed over and over. The crews rushed back to the safety of the ships. They could not believe their leader was dead.

Charles Clerke took over command of the *Resolution*. His place on the *Discovery* was given to a young officer.

Clerke demanded that Cook's body be returned. When it reached the ship, it was in pieces! Clerke was told that in the islands this was a mark of respect. He could do nothing but give Captain Cook an honored burial at sea.

Clerke could have gone straight home. Instead he vowed to try to find the Northwest Passage one more time. It was not a wise move. Men grew ill from the freezing weather. Clerke himself was sick. He managed to find someone to take Cook's journals and charts back to England. A few weeks later he, too, died.

The trip back to England was a nightmare. The ships ran into stormy weather and high seas. An active volcano near Iwo Jima covered the decks with ash and mud. At one stop they learned that France and Spain were at war with England. But there was good news. The warring countries agreed not to harm the *Resolution* or the *Discovery*. Their voyage had been too important.

It is hard to grasp how important Cook's voyages were to the world. He corrected the faulty maps the world had been using. He opened trade routes. He made life on board ship healthier for seamen everywhere. His reports caused New Zealand and Australia to become English colonies. It may be said that James Cook reshaped the world's knowledge of itself – and thus gave progress a mighty push forward.